Karen is the bestselling author of the *Indie Kidd* series, as well as other fiction for children and teenagers. She used to write for magazines *J17* and *Sugar*. Karen lives in London with her husband, small daughter and two fat cats.

Lydia Monks

won the Smarties Prize for *I Wish I Were a Dog*. She has illustrated many poetry, novelty and picture books for children, including the *Girl Zone* series for Walker Books. Lydia lives in Sheffield with her husband and daughter.

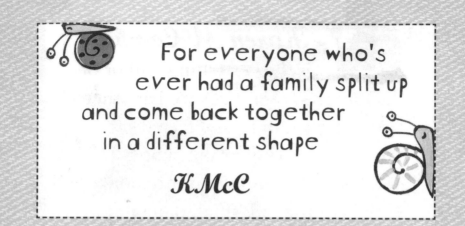

For everyone who's
ever had a family split up
and come back together
in a different shape
𝒦𝑀𝑐𝒞

First published 2007 by Walker Book Ltd
87 Vauxhall Walk, London SE11 5HJ

2 4 6 8 10 9 7 5 3 1

Text © 2007 Karen McCombie
Illustrations © 2007 Lydia Monks

The right of Karen McCombie and Lydia Monks to be identified as author
and illustrator respectively of this work has been asserted by them in accordance
with the Copyright, Designs and Patents Act 1988

This book has been typeset in Granjon

Printed and bound in Great Britain by
Creative Print and Design (Wales), Ebbw Vale

British Library Cataloguing in Publication Data:
a catalogue record for this book is available from the British Library

ISBN 978-1-4063-0078-9

www.walkerbooks.co.uk

KAREN McCOMBIE • LYDIA MONKS

My BIG (strange) Happy Family!

WALKER
BOOKS

The kind heart and the snail

I had to draw a map.

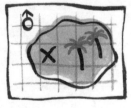

It wasn't a treasure map or anything exciting.

It wasn't a map of a country, like India, which I'm nearly – but not quite – named after. (I'm actually named after a dog called India, which might have been named after the country.)

The map I had to draw was a **family map**.

"Don't you mean a family tree?" my best friend Fee asked our teacher, Miss Levy, who was the one rabbitting on about maps.

"No," Miss Levy shook her head. "A **family map** is where you stick photos of everyone in your family who's important to you on a sheet of paper, and then write why they're important alongside."

Does that include pets? I wondered, thinking of my

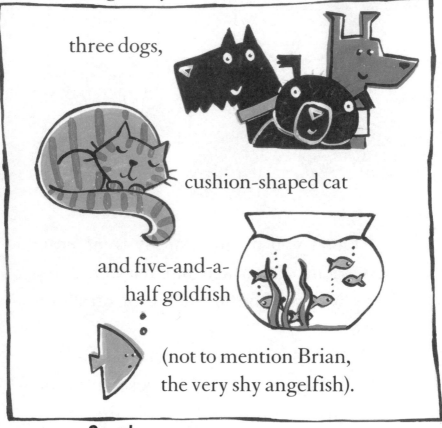

three dogs,

cushion-shaped cat

and five-and-a-half goldfish

(not to mention Brian, the very shy angelfish).

If **family maps** did include pets, I was going to need a very big sheet of paper.

"Now a family tree," Miss Levy continued, "is where you start with you, then trace back to as many ancestors as you can."

"What's a Nancestor?" asked Ayse Keçeli.

Fee rolled her eyes, which wasn't quite fair. OK, so Fee has a talent for knowing lots of excellently *looooong* words, but Ayse could only say "Hello" and "I don't speak English" when she moved here from Turkey last year. Now Ayse can say lots of different stuff, and if I'd been her I'd've said, "Don't roll your eyes at me, Fee, just 'cause I don't know what a Nancestor is!"

"It's like your great-great-great-great grandfather or whatever!" my other best friend, Soph, burst in.

(It's nice to have two best friends. You can never run out, even if one is off school sick.)

"Yes, that's right, Sophie," Miss Levy nodded. "An ancestor is someone in your family from a long time ago."

"Someone who's dead!" said Simon Green.

Simon Green likes talking about dead things. He especially likes talking about dead things to

girls in class, 'cause he knows it makes
them either

feel sick,

cry,

or

scream.

"Well, we're not doing anything about
ancestors today," said Miss Levy quickly,
ignoring the fact that Simon Green had his
hand up. (He probably wanted to share a
story about his great-great-great granny
getting squashed by a tram or something.)
Instead, Miss Levy, turned to me.

"Indie, can you help me out, please?"

Oh, good, I thought, as she headed for the cupboard. *We're going to get the TV out!* Watching TV in class is always the best. Well, it could be even better if Miss Levy came round and handed out ice-cream and popcorn too, but I didn't suppose that was going to happen (pity).

"This morning, we're going to watch a programme where children talk about who's important in their family," said Miss Levy, as she pulled out the TV stand and twisted it into position with my help. "And hopefully, it will give you all good ideas when it comes to doing your own **family map**."

"Can my map have **dead** people in it?" asked Simon Green.

"No!" said Miss Levy quite sternly. "Now for the next twenty minutes, I want everyone to concentrate. No talking, no shuffling, no fidgeting."

And no mentioning dead people, I guessed, as I made my way back to my seat.

But two steps from my table, I noticed a silvery something on the lino floor.

"All right, Indie?" asked Miss Levy.

I suddenly realized I'd stopped in mid-step, with one foot raised, like I was playing a one-person game of musical statues.

"Uh, yes," I said, nodding and restarting my legs.

I wanted to tell her about the silvery something.

I wanted to say that it had to be a snail trail.

I wanted to find the snail who'd left that trail, and rescue it before Simon Green or one of the other boys stood on it and it ended up squished on the sole of a trainer.

But as Miss Levy was in a "no talking, no shuffling, no fidgeting" mood, I didn't suppose she was in a snail rescuing mood either.

As I sat back down in my seat, Miss Levy flicked on the TV, and the programme started.

It was an interesting programme. For twenty minutes, no-one talked, shuffled or fidgeted; instead they watched and listened, and laughed if any children in the programme said anything funny.

Except for me.

I really tried to watch and listen (and I even started laughing when everyone else did, though I hadn't a clue what could be so funny). That's 'cause I had my eyes glued to the snail, who was slowly and dangerously slinking and slithering between chair legs, restless feet and school bags.

How did it get in? I fretted.

Then I saw the overgrown bush by the open window, and figured the snail had decided to climb up, come in and get itself educated.

How will it get out? I fretted some more.

I snuck a look at my watch: it would be break time soon. I got my legs poised, like a sprinter, so that at the very first *B* of the school bell's

briiiiinnnnngggggggg!!

I could lunge at the snail and scoop it up safely.

That's if it doesn't slink into someone's school bag or slither up Miss Levy's leg first, I fretted even more.

But while I was busy fretting, a very useful thing happened; the snail changed course and began slinking away from Ruby Nugent's lunchbox towards me instead.

It knew!

It knew deep down in its tiny snail heart that I was 100% animal mad, and that I'd inherited my mum's talent for rescuing animals (you don't get to be manageress for the *Paws For Thought* Animal Rescue Centre without being an ace rescuer!).

Or maybe the snail just knew that I was the only person in the class who wouldn't go "**Yuck!**" when they saw it...

It was very close now.

Close enough to reach down and grab it in my hand, where it could slime around inside my fist till I could set it free in the bushes at break time.

The next second, everyone, including Miss Levy, burst out laughing at something some kid on-screen said. Quick as I could, I bent down, scooped, and sat back up.

And not a second too soon.

"Well," smiled Miss Levy, switching off the TV and turning to face us all. "I'm sure that's given you all lots of inspiration for your **family maps**!"

Uh-oh.

Thanks to my kind heart and the snail that was ticklishly oozing round my palm, I'd missed every bit of inspiration going.

To use one of Fee's excellently *looooong* words, I was in a bit of a predicament.

Or a real **pickle**, if you wanted to use a short word of mine.

My small, happy family

True friends are very important.

True friends are always fun to hang out with.

True friends like you even when you're having a grumpy day.

True friends will let you know you when you have blue felt-pen on your nose, and won't let you walk about all day looking like a **dweeb**.

True friends explain your homework projects to you when you've been too busy fretting over lost snails to pay attention in class.

"On the TV programme, it showed you lots of different ways to do your **family map**," said Fee.

She was very carefully holding back a thorny bit of rosebush, so I could put the snail safely into the shrubbery by the school railings.

"You can put people in order of importance, like having a photo of your parents really big, and then everyone else's photos get smaller and smaller," Fee carried on. "Or you can link up all the photos with arrows, showing who is important to who. Stuff like that."

I stood up and waved goodbye to the snail, hoping he'd find some new snail buddies in this patch of plants, far away from open school windows.

"Yeah, and I've decided I'm going to do my map as a sort of flower," said Soph, drawing circular shapes in the air with her finger. "I'm going to put a photo of my granny in the middle, with me and all my cousins around her, like petals!"

"And I'm going to write little poems about everyone on my **family map**, just to make it more special!" Fee announced.

Hmm...

Maybe I could put a photo of me and Mum in the centre of my **family map**, and have all the pets dotted around us. But I didn't think I could come up with poems for them all.

(Brian, Brian,
My angelfish so shy.
I really like you lots,
Though you hide
when I say hi...)

"I don't know what I'm going to do to make mine special," I muttered, scratching my head. And remembering too late that my hand was covered in snail slime.

"Hey! I know, Indie!" said Soph excitedly. "You could use a photo of your mum from when she was a model!"

Me, Soph and Fee loved looking through Mum's old scrapbook. There were pictures of her pouting with lots of make-up on, wearing fancy clothes in magazines and walking down catwalks. She looked very pretty.

But I think she looks even better now, with no make-up, and khaki trousers covered in cat hair.

"I'm not sure..." I said. "Mum looking all glamorous wouldn't quite go with pictures of Dibbles and the goldfish."

"But pets can't be part of a **family map**!" Fee frowned at me. "It's just about people!"

"Oh. I didn't realize," I said, realizing that I really should have been paying more attention to Miss Levy and the TV programme. "But then my **family map** will end up being tiny – there's just going to be me and Mum!"

"And your dad!" laughed Fee.

"And Dylan!" laughed Soph.

Oops.

All that fretting over snails had made me forget about who was who in my family.

But OK, now that I was starting to get the hang of it, I had an idea for my **family map**: I could draw one house with me and Mum in it, and one house with Dad and my stepbrother Dylan in it.

Apart from writing something nice about everyone, I could also put something at the top about how my family lived in two different places but we all got along fine.

Yay!

Suddenly I wasn't in a pickle any more.

I might not have a very big family (like Soph's) but I had a happy one.

My small, happy family.

Yep, this homework project was going to be as easy-peasy as rescuing that snail.

"Indie," said Soph, standing on her tip-toes and peering over the bushes. "Isn't that your snail crawling through the rail-ings and heading for the road…?"

A slithery coincidence

"Hello!" I said, dumping my school bag down on the table.

Caitlin glanced up from whatever she was scribbling.

And – **ooh** – she was looking a bit, um, scary.

It's just as well she's a childminder for a not-easily-frightened ten-year-old like me. If she'd been looking after a toddler, they'd be starting to sob hysterically right about now.

"You look …
different," I said.

"I got braces
today," said Caitlin,
even though I couldn't
exactly miss them.

She was talking in a
very odd way, without her
lips meeting.

"Did the dentist say you had to … to
sort of smile that way?"

"No – they just feel weird. I'm too
scared to play my didgeridoo; I don't
know what that'll feel like…"

Wow. Caitlin not having her daily
parp on her didgeridoo… That was as
weird as the idea of Mum wearing
designer dresses and high heels instead of
khakis and wellies.

"Nice day at school?" Caitlin asked, in her new, odd way of talking.

"Yeah. I saved a snail."

(I wondered if the snail had made it safely to the other side of the main road yet, or if it had been squished by a number seventy-three bus.)

"Cool!" said Caitlin, though I had a feeling she wasn't really listening, now that she was scribbling something again.

"What are you doing?" I asked, getting off the subject of braces and possibly-squished snails.

Instead, I looked around at the scrawled-on yellow sticky notes dotted all around the kitchen.

"Well," said Caitlin, "when I was at the dentist, I read a really good article in this maga-zine–"

She held a page up.

"–about educational games you can play with children, so I thought we could do this!"

She stretched her arms out, to show off the sticky notes.

I took a step closer to the one that was stuck to the toaster.

It had the letter *P* on it in marker pen.

"What is it?"

I asked warily.

"It's an Alphabet Treasure Hunt!" Caitlin explained.

"Huh?"

"Well, you have to run round the house, collect all the stickies, and put them on the counter here in the correct order!"

Right behind her, I saw Dibbles pad his way in from the hall, with the letter *E* accidentally stuck to his wagging tail.

"But why?" I couldn't help asking.

"It'll help you learn the alphabet!"

"But I learnt the alphabet about five years ago!" I pointed out, noticing something in the magazine that Caitlin obviously hadn't. "See?"

EDUCATIONAL GAMES FOR YOUR FIVE-YEAR-OLD

was written at the top of the page.

"Oh... Um, sorry, Indie," said Caitlin, shrugging her shoulders. "Er ... can I help you with your homework or something instead?"

Poor Caitlin. She used to be a nanny for babies, and was very, very bad at it. She tried her best, but kept forgetting important stuff, like the fact that babies don't find loud rock music soothing.

"Yes," I said to her offer of help with my homework.

(Caitlin scrunched up the remaining pile of u, v, x, y and z sticky notes. Over by the bin, Dibbles was licking the letter r, just in case it tasted good.)

"I've got to do a **family map** thing. Can you take a photo of me for it?"

"Sure!" said Caitlin, in her funny, wide-mouthed way, as she rummaged around in a kitchen drawer and pulled out our camera.

"Er…"

"Er, what?" I asked Caitlin, relaxing my posed grin.

"Your hair's a bit strange, Indie. The fringe is all flat and stuck down at one side."

Ah, *snail slime*.

"Well, I've got till next Friday to do my map," I said with a shrug. "You can take my photo over the weekend."

And this weekend, I'd take some nice shots of Mum, Dad and Dylan. But I hadn't used the camera in ages, so I decided I'd better practise.

"Say cheese!" I ordered Caitlin, before snapping her in mid-mad mouth mode.

"Say woof!" I ordered Dibbles, Kenneth and George, before Dibbles licked the lens and left it covered in dog drool.

"Say miaow!" I ordered Smudge, who carried on sleeping.

"Say …
whatever fish say!" I ordered the goldfish and Brian, as they pootled around their tank.

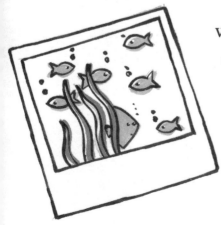

"Hey, stay right there!" I ordered Mum, as I suddenly spotted her through the lens.

She was coming through the kitchen door carrying something big; something heavy.

"Bit hard to do, Indie!" she said, still managing a quick smile for the click of the camera.

"What've you got today?" I asked her, sticking the camera down, and running to help her, along with Caitlin.

But as soon as Caitlin reached peeking-in distance of the tank, she jumped right back.

"Is it a tarantula again?" I asked.

Being our lodger, Caitlin is used to the strange assortment of furry or scaly things that Mum sometimes brings home from the centre to look after. The only time I ever saw her go funny was when the tarantula came to stay. ("It looks like a big hairy hand," she'd said with a shiver.)

"No, it's not spiders," said Mum, gently clunking the tank down on the kitchen worktop. "They're two Giant African Land Snails."

Wow – what a coincidence.

What a slithery coincidence.

And wow – compared to the normal, everyday snail I'd helped relocate at school today, these things were ginormous.

Imagine my Scottie, Kenneth, sitting next to a buffalo, and you get the difference in size.

"They're practically the size of my head!" I said, gazing at the enormous shells.

Caitlin gagged a bit, like she was thinking about being sick. Still, that was good – as she ran out of the room, I noticed that at least it had made her close her mouth properly.

"Is she all right? She seemed a bit peculiar," said Mum, who looked a bit peculiar too, with the paw prints of a tiny something on her cheek and her hair adorned with hamster bedding (as usual).

"She got a brace fitted today," I explained.

"I see. And what's with that?" she asked, nodding her head towards the camera, while picking up a Giant African Land Snail and smiling at it. (It was kind of hard to tell if it was smiling back.)

"I've got to do a project at school, about my family," I explained.

"So a photo of me is going to feature in your project, then?"

"Yep. Right in the middle of the **family map** I've got to do. Can I take some more?" I asked, picking up the camera again.

"Of course!" said Mum, beaming my way, while stroking the Land Snail. "Just as long as you don't get me to do any of those ridiculous poses your dad's so keen on..."

Dad is a wedding photographer. He likes to make his wedding photos special and unique, by taking the bride and groom at weird angles and stuff. Sadly, the brides and grooms don't really like their wedding photos taken at special, unique and weird angles. And neither did Mum, by the sound of it.

"I won't," I promised her, clicking away at a normal angle.

"And speaking about your dad; is he still all right to look after you tomorrow, since Caitlin's busy?" Mum asked, her camera-ready smile slipping away.

"Yep, think so."

"Hmm. He'd better be. I was sure he wasn't listening properly when I called and talked to him about it. I could hear him playing around with the shutter of his camera in the background…"

Mum's face was the opposite of smiley now.

And that's when something not-very-nice popped into my head.

As far as I could remember, Mum never smiled when she spoke about my dad. I mean never. And now I thought about it, Dad didn't exactly break into beaming smiles at the mention of Mum's name.

Which made me wonder suddenly about my supposed small, happy family.

I mean, I knew for sure that Mum and Dad didn't love each other any more, and that was OK.

But did they even like each other?

4

(Not) for ever and ever and ever

Saturday is the busiest day of the week for Mum.

It's the day lots of (fingers-crossed) new owners come to the *Paws For Thought* Animal Rescue Centre to look for a pet.

And Saturday is the busiest day of the week for my dad too.

Although people do get married on other days, Saturday is a total confetti-throwing wedding-fest.

But today, he wasn't just taking arty wedding photos; he was looking after me (see, he had been listening, Mum!) and my stepbrother Dylan too.

And in-between Dad asking the wedding party to do a Mexican wave, and fitting fancy lenses on his camera that made the bride glow like she was radioactive, I wanted to talk to him about Mum.

Yesterday, Mum's face had fallen when she mentioned him; now I wanted to test Dad and see if his face did an identical fall when I mentioned Mum.

In the meantime, me and Dylan were hovering by a very big, very grand, old gravestone, trying to keep out of Dad's way while he worked.

"So what do people do on a didgeridoo course?" Dylan asked.

Caitlin often looks after me on a Saturday, but today she was meeting up with lots of other didgeridoo players in the town hall. (I don't know if they were handing out earplugs to passers-by.)

"Um, they just learn to play new tunes, I suppose," I answered, thinking that all songs played on a didgeridoo sound the same, in a rumbly, boomy, gloomy kind of way. "She's a bit nervous – she's got a brace and doesn't know if she can play that well."

"Why do people get braces, Indie?" asked Dylan.

Did I ask as many questions as Dylan when I was nine? I don't think so. Our brains don't work the same way. Dylan's brain is like a slightly annoying computer.

"To make their teeth straight," I replied.

"Why do people need to have their teeth straight?"

Sometimes Dylan asks questions that I don't have the answers to.

"Dunno. Anyway, what kind of course is Fiona doing this weekend?"

OK, my turn for a question, even if it was just to stop Dylan asking them for a bit. Though I was kind of curious to know what my stepmum was up to: she's the cooking editor of the local newspaper, and was bound to be teaching people something very yummy.

"She's teaching people how to ice cakes," said Dylan, as we stepped aside for a bunch of bridesmaids who

Dad had asked to skip across the lawn.

"That's nice," I replied, wondering if the oldest, quite plump bridesmaid was going to hit Dad with her bouquet for making her do something so stupid.

"Indie, why do cakes need to be iced?"

See what I mean about Dylan's questions being hard to answer sometimes? I mean, why should people's teeth be straight – they still work when they're a bit wonky, don't they? And why should cakes be iced? You just pick the icing off and leave the cake after all…

"I don't know. Maybe—"

"And why do brides and bridesmaids have to wear long, fluffy dresses?" Dylan carried on with his hard-to-answer questions, not really bothering to wait for me to try and answer any more. "Is there a rule? Is it like school uniform?"

"Well, I—"

"And why do people get married anyway?"

Ah ... I knew the answer to this one.

"'Cause it shows everyone that you love each other enough to want to be together for ever and ever and ever," I told him.

"Well, why didn't your mum and dad stay together for ever and ever and ever?"

Dylan and his hard-to-answer questions: they were starting to give me a headache.

"You two all right?" said Dad

cheerfully, as he came over to grab a different camera out of his bag.

"Yes, Dad," I answered him, though I
didn't feel very all right. I suddenly had a
big sad something in my tummy.

"Mike?"

"Yes, Dylan?" said Dad, gazing up.

"Why didn't you stay married to Indie's mum for ever and ever and ever?" Dylan blurted out.

Subtle is a new word that Fee has been using. *Subtle* means doing something in a quiet way, that no one notices.

Dylan is not subtle.

"Ahem!" Dad coughed, going a bit red at this direct question. "Well! Um, India's mum and I loved each other very much at first. But … um … then we didn't!"

I saw him glancing at me, all of a fluster.

"But we will both always love India, of course!"

Then I saw him glancing all of a fluster at Dylan.

"And I love you and your mum, of course!"

The bride and groom were just behind Dad, looking

a) a bit fed-up
b) at their watches

I guess they needed Dad to hurry up with the photos so they could get on with the eating, drinking and dancing part of their wedding.

So if I wanted to find out how Dad felt about Mum, I needed to ask him right now.

"Dad?"

"Yes, Indie?" he said, a trickle of sweat running down his forehead, like he was a bit worried I was going to ask him another tricky question.

And I was.

"But you and Mum are friends, right?"

For about a sixteenth of a second, Dad pulled a face like he'd accidentally just sucked a lemon. Then he realized what that must look like and put on a pretend happy smile.

"Of course!" he lied. "Right, better get going – got to get the bride and groom waltzing round the rhododendrons…"

Humphhh.

How could I do a nice **family map** if the two most important people on it weren't even friends?!

There was only one thing for it.

I was going to have to think of *some way* to make them like each other – whether they liked it or not.

5

The friends-
or-not test

It was Sunday morning, and Mum was having a very special soak in the bath.

It was special because I'd thrown in the flower-petal bath bomb I'd got for my tenth birthday from Soph.

I'd also piled up some magazines on the toilet seat (*Wildlife In Focus*, *Pets And You*, *Lizards Today*).

I'd even made a fruit cocktail (orange juice, with a hunk of melon and a blackcurrant thrown in).

And I'd told Mum she wasn't allowed
to come out for at least an hour.

I think Mum thought I was trying to
win the Good Daughter Awards.

But really, I just wanted an out-of-
Mum's-radar chat with Caitlin.

"So what do you think?" I asked her, now that I'd blurted what was running through my head.

"I think they are seriously, seriously creepy," said Caitlin, from the other side of the kitchen.

"**What?!**" I frowned. "My mum and dad?!"

I thought Caitlin really liked Mum! And I know she didn't know him so well, but what was so wrong with my dad?"

"No! Not your Mum and Dad!"

(Caitlin had stopped talking with her lips wedged apart, but was now speaking with her lips very exaggerated, as if she was helping out someone who was learning to lip-read.)

"What, then?" I asked. I wasn't used to Caitlin making my head go spinny. That was Dylan's job.

"Those **evil snail thingies**!" Caitlin said with a shudder.

Ah, she was talking about the Giant African Land Snails. We were cleaning their tank (OK – *I* was cleaning their tank) while Mum was having her very special Sunday morning soak in the bath.

"They are not evil snail thingies!" I protested.

Though they did look kind of weird and out-of-proportion just now. While I de-scuzzed their tank, I'd put them in an old glass pudding bowl with a plate stuck on top so they couldn't escape.

And something about the thick glass of the pudding bowl did sort of distort their strange little horn/feeler thingamajigs.

"Yes they are," Caitlin insisted. "When I came in here to make toast this morning, those things were staring at me, in this really creepy way!"

"For a start, I don't think they've got very good eyesight," I said, standing up for the snails. "And secondly, they are not 'those things'. They are called Fleur and Amélie."

Those were the names their former owner had given them. I had no idea which of the identical snails was Fleur, and which was Amélie. But with names as pretty as that, they couldn't be described as "creepy".

"Well, I still don't like them," said Caitlin, folding her arms across her chest.

"Well, I still don't like the fact that you haven't listened to what I was saying about Mum and Dad!" I told her back.

"Yes, I have! And I've been thinking about it too. I'll show you."

To prove her point, Caitlin went over to the chair where Smudge the cat was sleeping, and gently pulled out an older teenage magazine from under her.

"Look!" said Caitlin, holding a page up (at a safe distance) for me to see.

HOW TO WEAR BLUSHER THIS SEASON

I read out loud, feeling very confused.

How was that going to help Mum and Dad like each other again?

"Oops!" giggled Caitlin, quickly flicking to another page.

CAN YOU STAY FRIENDS WITH YOUR EX?

I read out this time. "**Cool!** So what does it
say?"

"Well," Caitlin began, scanning the
page. "There's this test here. It says you
think of three things you liked about your
ex, and three things you didn't. If you
think of the nice things really quickly, you
probably could still be friends. But if you
think of the bad things really easily…"

Caitlin didn't have to explain any more.
I needed to try out the friends-or-not test
on Mum straight away.

"Hello, honey!" she smiled, flicking her dozing eyes open. "What's that?"

Mum had only been in her very special Sunday morning bath for fifteen minutes when I barged in on her, armed with the magazine.

"It's something just for fun," I said.

Mum looked a bit perplexed. Maybe I

should have said what I just said in a **fun** sort
of voice, instead of a solemn sort of voice.

"Think of when you and Dad were
together," I ordered her.

"Do I have to?" Mum said, pulling a
jokey face.

Uh-oh – I suspected this might not go
very well.

"Yes you have to. Now, can you think of three things you liked about him?"

"What's this about, Indie?" asked Mum, over the top of a pile of petal-speckled bubbles.

"Just say, Mum. It's just for fun," I told her, knowing my voice still sounded a bit, well, no-fun.

"Well, I guess he was ... let me see..."

It took Mum nearly four minutes to come up with:

> He was quite funny.
>
> He used to sometimes buy me crisps as a surprise.
>
> He had nice hair.

"Now say three things you didn't like about him."

> He bit his nails.
>
> He always forgot to put CDs back in their cases so they got scratched.
>
> He wasn't really into animals.

It took her four seconds flat to say that lot.

Uh-oh, big-time.

Fast forward to two hours later.

'Cause two hours later, I was at my regular Sunday lunch with Dad.

Only it wasn't quite the regular Sunday lunch. Because Fiona was doing her weekend "How To Ice Cakes" class somewhere, me, Dad and Dylan were having lunch at the café in the park, instead of at Dad's house.

This was quite nice, for a change.

I mean, I missed Fiona's most excellent cooking, but since we'd come to the park, it meant I could bring the dogs with me too.

And I could never bring the dogs to Fiona and Dad's house, 'cause Fiona (pretty nice as she is) is allergic to the mess animals make, like shedded hair and stuff.

"What's that, then, Indie?" asked Dad,

as I dragged Caitlin's magazine out of my bag and flopped it on the wooden picnic table.

"I'm going to ask you a couple of questions now," I told him.

"Ooh! Sounds exciting, doesn't it, Dylan?" said Dad, smiling at my stepbrother, who was currently feeding each of the three dogs salt 'n' vinegar crisps, one by one.

"I like questions. Can I help?" said Dylan, glancing up.

"No!" I said quickly. "They're just for Dad!"

Dylan frowned at me, wondering why I was sounding stern as a grumpy teacher.

"Um ... fire away, then!" said Dad, glancing from me to Dylan and back again.

"Try to remember back when you and Mum were together."

"Help! No! Don't make me!!" Dad joked about, thinking he was being funny.

Then he checked out my not-laughing face and gave a little cough.

Not-laughing face

"Ahem. Sorry. So, what about it?"

"Well," I began again, "thinking back, can you remember three things you really liked about her?"

"Let's see… She was very clever. And I loved the way she dressed up in amazing clothes all the time."

Two very speedy answers. So far so good for Dad's test scores.

"As for a third thing…"

Dad stared into space for about *five years*.

He was taking so long that I felt like prodding him with a big stick.

The way he was going it would be bedtime for me and Dylan before long.

"ORDER NUMBER TEN?" a waitress suddenly bellowed, coming out of the café with a piled-high tray. "Who ordered jacket potatoes and beans?"

"Ah, that's us!" said Dad, sounding relieved to be set free from his task. "I'd better stand up and give the waitress a wave so she knows where we are—"

That was the sound of Dad standing up, taking a step forward, and falling straight over Dibbles.

"Aargh! My ankle!!" he yelped from somewhere under a pile of suddenly very concerned dogs.

The test hadn't just proved that Mum and Dad really weren't friends; it had also caused my dad actual bodily harm!

Still … it wasn't all bad news.

Maybe fate had stepped (tripped?) in to help me out.

Suddenly there was a very obvious way to try to get Mum and Dad closer together.

My evil genius plan (minus the evil bit)

Hospitals are very strange places.

People have very strange conversations in them.

Mooching around in the waiting room – while Dad got his ankle X-rayed – me and Dylan heard loads of odd snatches of conversation going on.

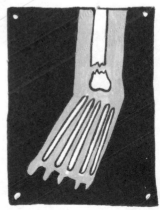

75

One lady was on the phone, explaining that her husband had been diagnosed with streptacockles. (I didn't know what that was exactly but it didn't sound good.)

"That'll teach you to play with a sieve!" a mum grumpily told her little kid. (The kid looked sheepish, but I couldn't see any obvious sieve-related injuries.)

A very serious-looking doctor leant over and asked the receptionist if she knew what fruit started with a *p*, ended in an *e* and had eleven letters in it. (If I'd been in the mood, I could've helped him with his crossword. The answer was

We did a project on fruit at school last term.)

And now me and Dylan were having a strange conversation of our own. Dylan was doing his usual thing of asking a *zillion* different questions at once, but changing subjects just to keep me well and truly muddled.

DO you think your dad's ankle is just twisted, or broken?

"I don't know. I guess we'll find out from the X-ray."

How do X-rays work?

"I don't know."

(The same way as electricity, digital TV and the Internet, I supposed: by magic.)

How little were you when your dad moved out?

"Little. Before I can remember stuff."

Why do brides carry bouquets? Why don't they carry soft toys, or bags of sweets or something?

"I'm not sure. I guess flowers are prettier than soft toys or sweets."

"But lots of sweets are nice colours and pretty. And you can eat them!"

Boy, Dylan sure was babbling today. Maybe he was just in shock from having to clamber in the back of an ambulance with Dad. Still, he'd had a nice ride to the hospital, while I'd had to run here with three excitable dogs whose leads kept tangling up.

"How big are they?"

"How big are what?" I frowned.

"The Giant African Land Snails," Dylan prattled on.

"About that big," I said, making a shape with my hands.

I wished Dylan would be quiet for just a couple of minutes, so my brain wouldn't overheat. While I had the chance, I glanced out of the window at the entrance to the hospital.

I wasn't just looking at the dogs, tied up and tangled round a railing. I was watching out for Mum, who should be rushing here any second now...

"Are there normal sized ones too?"

"Are there normal sized whats?"

"Normal sized snails!"

"Where?" I said, wondering if Dylan was talking about the marigolds outside that Dibbles was currently weeing on.

"In Africa. Or do they just have giant ones?"

Maybe I could take Dylan to the Ear, Nose and Throat department and leave him there for a bit. I could tell them he had a rare condition called Babble-itus.

"I don't know what sizes of snails they have in Africa," I answered him wearily.

"Indie, why were you asking your dad all those questions in the park café?"

OK.

Now I had a question I could answer.

"It was a test. I tried it on Mum too. I wanted to see if they still liked each other."

"Why?" frowned Dylan.

"Because they're my mum and dad and I'd really like them to like each other!" I explained.

"And do they?"

"Like each other? They didn't score too high in the test, so I don't think they do. **Yet.**"

When I said that "yet", I felt my eyes light up, the

way evil genius' eyes do in movies when
they say stuff like,

And then I will take
over the WORLD!!
Mwa-ha-ha!

"What do you mean, 'yet'?" asked
Dylan, looking faintly worried. (Maybe he
was worried that his stepsister was turning
into an evil genius.)

"I've got a plan…"

Actually, that sounded like the sort of
thing an evil genius would say too.

"What are you going to do?" asked
Dylan, with a hint of a seriously worried
frown hovering above his eyebrows.

"I've done it already!"

"Done what?" asked Dylan, glancing around nervously for signs of something dramatic.

"I phoned my mum on the way over here and told her Dad had an accident."

Dylan relaxed a bit. I guess he might've suddenly thought that my evil genius plan (minus the evil bit) was a bit pants.

"Well, he has, Indie!"

"Yeah, I know," I nodded. "But I exaggerated some stuff."

"Like?"

"Like I told her he might have broken both legs. And – and that he was in a little bit of a coma."

"But he wasn't in a coma!" Dylan protested. "He was having tea and biscuits before they wheeled him to the X-ray!"

"Yes, but that's not the point, is it?"

Dylan blinked at me, his computer brain trying to make sense of what I was telling him.

"Look, I had to exaggerate so Mum would get all worried and realize she does care about him! And he will be so glad to know that she cares about him, that he'll really like her for caring!"

I'd hoped Dylan would say something like, "**cool idea!**", but instead he kept doing that blinking thing.

"Ah – here she comes now!" I beamed, spotting Mum hurtling out of the Rescue Centre van and hurrying into the entrance, pausing for only a millisecond to pat the dogs on the head.

Wow, this was such an excellent plan, I could practically hug myself.

"Indie," I heard Dylan say, as I waved at Mum to show her where we were.

"What?" I said distractedly.

"Isn't your mum going to be really cross with you, when she sees that your dad is only a bit hurt?"

OOpS.

I hadn't thought about that.

I guess that was the slight hitch in my not-very-evil genius plan.

"Indie! Dylan! Are you two all right? Don't worry Dylan, I've called your mum; she's on her way. Where's your father? Where's a doctor I can speak to?" Mum chattered furiously, as she hugged us both tight.

Gulp!

A huge amount of crossness

It was Monday morning. I was at school. Which was a much safer place to be than at home, where Mum was still growling at me.

"Was she really, really cross with you?" asked Soph, wide-eyed.

We were in the playground, comparing our weekends before the nine o'clock bell rang.

Soph had won third place in an Irish dancing competition.

Fee had spent the whole time doing her **family map**, and had finished it already, even though it wasn't due in till Friday.

And of course I'd had a plan to make my parents realize they liked each other deep down, which had spectacularly failed. They still didn't particularly like each other, and now I didn't think they particularly liked me either.

"No – Mum's not really, really cross with me," I said, shaking my head. "She's really, really, really, REALLY cross with me!"

I got a very *stern* lecture on the way home from the hospital yesterday. Mum had told me very *sternly* that she was really, really, really, REALLY cross with me for several reasons:

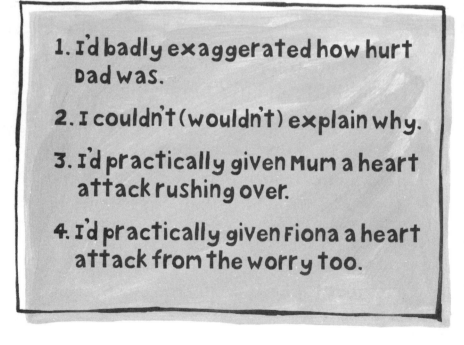

1. I'd badly exaggerated how hurt Dad was.

2. I couldn't (wouldn't) explain why.

3. I'd practically given Mum a heart attack rushing over.

4. I'd practically given Fiona a heart attack from the worry too.

I felt especially bad about Fiona. Mum had contacted her at her cooking course to tell her the (false) bad news.

Fiona had not only got scared stiff, but she'd left a bunch of students with icing bags poised and no idea what they were doing.

Which made Fiona and Dad pretty cross with me too.

Knowing all that huge amount of crossness was directed at me made me feel a bit sick.

"Has your dad got his leg in plaster?" asked Fee, changing the subject not much.

"No – since his ankle was only twisted, he's just got some stretchy bandage thing on it," I told her. "But he's got to be only crutches for a week to give it a rest."

Poor Dad. I didn't know how he was going to manage to do his job while balancing on crutches. He might have to tie his camera to his head or something. He might have to ask passers-by to snap the pictures for him.

"So what are you going to do next?" asked Soph. "How are you going to make them like each other now?"

"I don't know," I mumbled sadly.

Getting photos for my **family map** wasn't going to be a problem, but finding the right words would be. I couldn't bear the fact that I was going to have to write:

This is Mum. She is mad on animals, but not too keen on my dad.

This is Dad. He takes wedding photos, but wasn't too keen on being married to my mum.

"You've got to think of some-thing to get them to be friends again!" said Fee.

She was trying to think of something too, I could tell. She always twirls her long red curls round her fingers when she's doing some serious thinking.

"I'd better just leave it for a while," I said gloomily, since I'd caused enough damage.

"No! I mean, if it's making you unhappy, Indie, then you've got to keep trying," said Fee. "Can't you wangle it so they're left alone, and can just have a nice conversation together?"

"How's that going to happen?" I shrugged.

Whenever Dad dropped me off at my house, there was always me or Caitlin or the dogs or assorted giant

94

snails, tree frogs or baby hedgehogs around.

And whenever Mum picked me up at Dad's house, there was always Dylan and Fiona.

"Maybe you could get them talking by text!" suggested Soph.

"Yeah, but how could I get them to text each other in the first place?"

"I know!" said Fee, who'd been thinking so hard she'd completely tangled her fingers in her curls. "You send your dad a text first, pretending to be your mum!"

"Huh? What d'you mean?" I said with a frown.

"It's obvious!" said Fee. (It wasn't.) "You send a text, pretending to be your mum; your dad thinks it's genuine and answers back, then your mum answers back for real, and hey presto – they're having a proper conversation!"

Briiiiinnnnngggggggg!!

My head was buzzing; not just 'cause I was standing right beside the bell when it rang, but because Fee's idea was actually pretty good.

All morning, while Miss Levy went on about maths and history and other stuff I was only half-listening to, I thought about the text thing, and what I could say.

And then the right words hit me in an unexpected place.

Hey Mike. Soz about yesterday. Don't know what Indie was up to. Hope your leg gets better v.soon. Lynne xxx'

That's what I finally tapped into my phone at break-time, while I was sitting on the loo.

"Indie – you in there?" Fee's voice called out from the other side of the cubicle door.

"Coming in a second!" I called back, hitting the "send" key.

Hooray — my message was pinging its way to Dad. Now I'd just have to wait and see what happened.

Except...

Except a little niggle of doubt suddenly wriggled its way into my chest.

1. Mum wouldn't say "soz".

2. And Mum wouldn't put kisses at the end of a text.

3. Come to think of it, Mum didn't know how to text.

Maybe I'd rushed into doing this...

"Why are you taking so long, Indie?" Fee demanded to know.

"I was just sending that text off to Dad; the one that's meant to be from my mum!" I called back.

"Huh? But you can't send it from *your* phone! You've got to get hold of your mum's mobile and text from that! He'll see straight away it's from you!"

Eeeek!

Of course my name would leap up on his display!

Of course he would see straight away it was me, pretending to be Mum!

Of course he was going to think his one and only daughter was going quietly round the twist!

Bleep! went an incoming text on my phone.

I could barely bear to look.

```
Indie - I don't get that last
   message. What's going on?
```

I read through the gaps in my fingers as I covered my face in shame...

Muddled
from shock

Now Fee was cross with me.

I couldn't blame her, but I'd hoped she'd understand the little white lie I'd had to tell.

The little white lie where I'd explained to Dad that Fee had been fooling around with my phone and sent him that message as a dumb prank.

But what else could I do? I was in enough trouble with Mum and Dad as it was.

"Hello! I'm home!" I called out, as I opened the front door.

"Hi, honey!" Mum said cheer-fully, as she padded down the stairs.

Phew.

She seemed in a better mood. From the look of Kenneth, George and Dibbles – who were dripping their way around the hall – I guessed that Mum had spent her day off shampooing pups. (Doing anything with animals was always guaranteed to cheer her up.)

"Can you dry off Kenneth?" she asked, chucking me an old towel.

Dry, Kenneth looked like a sturdy little dog.

Wet, he looked like a semi-drowned meerkat.

"Did Dibbles try to eat the shampoo bottle again?" I asked Mum, as we both got down on our knees and rubbed soggy doggies.

"He tried, but I gave him the sponge to chew instead," she said with a shrug. "It's not very nutritious, but at least it won't give him a bad tummy like the shampoo."

This was nice, just chatting to Mum about dogs and their dodgy eating habits, instead of feeling the weight of her cross-ness.

"Have you just been hanging out with the pets today?" I asked her.

"Mmm. A photographer was meant to be coming from the newspaper today. But  it got blown out because someone set fire to three bins in the park, and they thought that was way more exciting than two enormous snails in need of a new home."

Mum pops up in the local newspaper nearly as regularly as Fiona in her cooking column, or Dad's wedding photos. She smiles in that pretty way of hers, while stroking whatever animal she's finding difficult to re-home.

It usually works.

People who were all set to buy a cute kitten get sidetracked by her photo, and her description of how fantastic that day's pet is, and next thing they're the proud owner of a newt.

"Will it be hard to find new homes for Fleur and Amélie?"

I knew the answer was yes (most little kids weren't likely to pester their parents for a humungous pet snail), but I was really enjoying having a normal conversation with Mum.

Maybe she wouldn't ever mention the thing with Dad and the hospital ever again...

"Indie," said Mum, suddenly glancing up at me, "I don't want to keep harping on about this, but why did you make out that  your dad was so badly injured yesterday?"

"I got muddled," I answered, feeling red-faced and muddled.

"Muddled?" Mum frowned.

"Muddled from shock," I carried on, hoping I sounded convincing.

I'm sure I didn't. It's not like characters on any of those hospital shows on telly ever say stuff like, "She's suffering from a terrible case of muddled-from-shock, doctor!".

But before Mum could quiz me any further, two pretty terrible, pretty loud noises got in the way.

One was the sound of some out-of-tune didgeridoo-ing (maybe the braces were making a difference after all).

The other was Dibbles, howling madly along with the didgeridoo.

"Urgh… I'm going to have to ask her to give it a rest," Mum sighed, getting up and heading towards Caitlin's room. "The neighbours will think we're torturing whales in here…"

As Mum knocked, and then disappeared into Caitlin's room for a chat, I clamped my hand round Dibbles' snout to shut him up.

In the sudden silence, an idea pinged into my head.

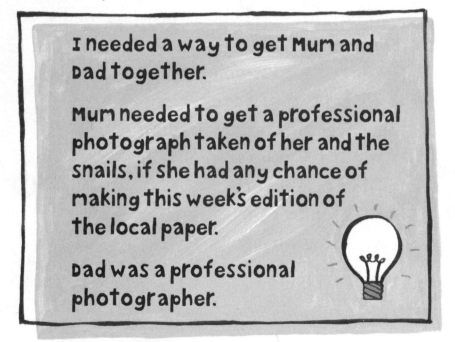

I needed a way to get Mum and Dad together.

Mum needed to get a professional photograph taken of her and the snails, if she had any chance of making this week's edition of the local paper.

Dad was a professional photographer.

See where my plan was going?

"Dad!"

"Indie?" said Dad, after taking a very long time to answer the phone. "What's up?"

"Mum needs a favour – now! Fleur and Amélie need a new home, and the photographer from the newspaper is at the bins on fire!"

There was silence from the other end of the line for a second. I think Dad was trying to decode the stream of gibberish I'd just wittered.

"Who are Fleur and Amélie?" he asked.

"Snails. Big ones."

My heart was pitter-pattering.

Please say you'll come and take their photo! I silently willed him. When he was here, I could disappear off to Caitlin's room, so Mum and Dad could be alone (with the snails) and chat. I'd even take the dogs, so they wouldn't howl or sniff or interrupt in a hairy way.

"I see. But I'm sorry — I can't help, Indie! With my leg like this, I can't drive over, and I can't really operate my camera while I'm on crutches."

"Oh. OK," I mumbled, feeling deflated.

"Tell your mum I'm sorry."

"I will," I said flatly, knowing I wouldn't. Mum didn't need to know about this next failed plan to get my parents together.

After saying bye, I knew there was nothing for it.

I'd just have to get on with my **family map** as it was.

And maybe Miss Levy would take pity on me and give me a special star for it being the Most Gloomy **family map** in the class.

The spitting image of a snail

Dylan was in the kitchen.

He'd cycled over after school today, desperate to meet the Giant African Land Snails.

He was wearing deely-boppers.

Don't ask…

"Trying to get Mum all concerned about Dad at the hospital – that didn't work," I sighed.

The deely-boppers – two silver balls on the end of long springs – wobbled as Dylan shook his head.

"Then I totally messed up that texting idea of Fee's."

The deely-boppers randomly wibbled about some more, in the air above my step-brother's head.

"And then yesterday, I thought it would be ace if Dad came and helped Mum by taking photos of Fleur and Amélie." (I'd decided that Fleur was the snail with the slightly darker shell.) "But he couldn't come, 'cause of his leg."

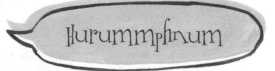

Hurummphnum

(That was Dibbles, making an apologetic noise. I guess he was still feeling guilty about tripping Dad up. Or maybe he was just confused by the sight of the wibbly deely boppers.)

"I really don't know how to get them together," I sighed again. "What about Fiona and your dad? Are they friends, Dylan?"

The deely-boppers bobbed around again.

"Dad moved to Tasmania when I was a baby, so they don't exactly get the chance to meet up too often," said Dylan, his eyes fixed on the huge snail currently oozing up his left arm.

Tasmania… Tasmania… I tried to picture a map of the world in my head, but couldn't figure out where it was exactly.

Instead, I filed it in a box in my brain marked "Very, Very Far Away Places", alongside Kuala Lumpur, Oz and Venus.

"She likes me!" Dylan beamed, as Amélie paused on his T-shirt sleeve and wiggled her feelers in the direction of his face.

"Before you say anything," I warned him, "she does not think you're another snail!"

"She does! I knew these would work."

Dylan reached up and tried to touch his "look-alike" feelers, but the silver bobbles kept Sproinging out of his grasp.

"But if you were me, Dylan, and your dad lived closer than Tasma-wotsit, how would you get your parents together?" I asked, steering the conversation away from stupid headgear and back to what was important.

Dylan's mind might work in a slightly slanted way (you only had to check out the deely-boppers to know that), but sometimes he came up with surprisingly surprising ideas.

Er...

Dylan acted like he hadn't heard me, and kept staring at Amélie.

"Dylan?"

Silence.

Did Amélie have special powers? Had she hypnotized my step-brother?

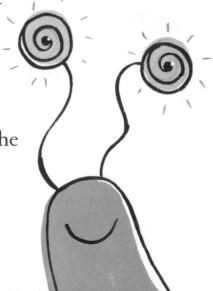

Just as I started to wave my hand in front of his face, Caitlin and her braces slouched into the kitchen.

"Now that is a great photo for your **family map**, Indie!" she half-laughed, half-winced, pointing at Dylan, his deely-boppers, and the snail sliming onto his shoulder. "Get the camera, quick!"

Dylan glanced up at Caitlin as she talked and flinched. If only she'd talk normally, and not as if her mouth was a letter-box.

"OK, Dylan – look over here!" I ordered him, as I grabbed the camera and clicked.

"I've got to go," said Dylan, suddenly going.

I didn't know why Dylan was leaving in such a hurry, but then I didn't really know how the inside of Dylan's strange mind worked most of the time.

"If you think of anything to get Mum and Dad together, you'll call me, right?" I said to him, as he scooped up his schoolbag from the table.

"OK," he nodded, deelies bopping.

Caitlin took a step back, to get out of his way. Well, to get out of the way of his slithery friend, more like.

"Hey, are you taking Amélie?" I asked, as he headed for the hallway. (He'd get a few looks if he tried cycling home with a pair of deely-boppers on his head and a Giant African Land Snail slimed to his shoulder…)

"Oh," murmured Dylan. "Uh, no. Sorry."

Poor Caitlin. Like me, she probably thought he'd turn back, and carefully put Amélie into her tank. Or at least, turn back, and hand her to me.

Instead, seeing she was closer, Dylan gently but speedily grabbed Amélie by the shell and deposited her in Caitlin's hands.

There was a stunned silence for a second, broken only by the sound of the front door closing.

And then…

Eeeeeeeeeeeeeeee
eeeeeeeeeeee!!!

I quickly tried to plop Fleur back in her tank, but she had other ideas. She was suctioned to my hand like an octopus using superglue.

"I'm coming!" I called out over my shoulder. "Just take a long, deep, slow breath!"

Caitlin was standing frozen, a look of pure panic on her face, as Dibbles wandered casually over and gave Amélie a sniff.

Uh-oh. The sight of a big, black animal getting way too close must have been terrifying for a snail, even a giant one. Immediately, Amélie recoiled her feelers and slunk back into her shell.

"That feels seriously weird," said Caitlin, in the most wibbly-wobbly of voices. "What's it doing?"

"She's scared," I explained, as I still struggled to ease Fleur off my hand. "She probably thinks Dibbles is a black panther, come to eat her for a snack."

I know, I know. Dibbles looks more like a back bin liner filled with soup than a panther, but like I say, snails don't have great eyesight.

"It's scared?" said Caitlin, suddenly sounding less scared herself.

"Uh-huh," I nodded, finally feeling Fleur ooze off.

When I turned round this time, I saw something I hadn't quite expected ten seconds ago. And I heard a completely different kind of noise coming from Caitlin.

"**Awwww…**" she crooned softly, holding the snail up for closer inspection. "Don't be frightened!"

Caitlin and Amélie… Who'd have guessed they could get on?

It gave me a warm **fuzzy** feeling inside.

A warm fuzzy feeling of hope.

If slither-phobic Caitlin and a Giant African Land Snail could be friends, maybe I shouldn't give up on Mum and Dad just yet!

10
A slimy emergency

"Smile!"

It was Wednesday, i.e. two days till I had to hand in my **family map**.

I'd come round to Dad's after school, to take a photo of him, since I hadn't managed to before now.

(I'd had the camera with me in the park on Sunday, but twisted ankles and urgent trips to the hospital kind of got in the way.)

"How's this?" asked Dad.

Through the lens, I could see a faraway  Dad sitting on the sofa, and some close-up toes wiggling at me.

"Dad! You're supposed to be resting it!" I told him off, pointing for him to put his blue-bandaged leg back down on the stool.

"But I'm bored!" Dad moaned cheerfully. "I'm just not very good at sitting still!"

"Well, you've got to. Mum said that a dog at the Rescue Centre had a sore leg and it kept bouncing about, so it took ages to heal!"

"Did she now?" said Dad.

"Yes – she told me that today, when I was talking about coming to see you. And she said to say she hoped you felt better."

Oops, a bit of a white lie (or two) there.

I mean, Mum did say the thing about the dog, only it was about two months ago. And when I mentioned I was coming to  see Dad for my project after school today, instead of sending a get-well-soon message what she'd actually said was, "Fine. Can you pick up some milk on your way home, please?"

"Well, that's nice. Now where's that Dylan got to? Isn't it time you were pestering him for a photo?" said Dad, trying to scratch an itch inside his tight bandage.

I hadn't seen Dylan since I arrived.

"I'll go ask Fiona where he is," I offered, thinking that I might also be allowed to nibble whatever cookies she seemed to be making at the same time.

"And you'll be taking her photo for

your project too, won't you, Indie?"

"Of course!" I replied brightly.

Wow, what a lot of white lies I was telling today.

I hadn't thought of taking Fiona's photo for my project at all. But of course it would be silly to miss her out of my **family map**, since she was:

> 1. Married to Dad
> 2. My stepmum
> 3. The maker of very excellent-smelling cookies.

"Have you seen Dylan?" I asked, as I wandered into the kitchen.

"Um … not for a while, actually," Fiona frowned.

129

The kitchen table was neatly arranged with bowls and rolling pins and eggs and stuff. Nothing – including Fiona – was the tiniest bit messy.

When I try and make cakes, it ends up looking like I've had a wrestling match with a bag of flour.

"I'll check his room in a second," I told her. "But can I take your photo first, for my **family map**?"

"Yes! What would you like me to do?" beamed Fiona, looking delighted at being included in my project.

I thought for a second.

Just as Mum didn't look right without hamster bedding in her blonde hair, my stepmum didn't look right without a mixing spoon in her hand.

"Can you pick up the bowl and pretend to stir something?" I asked her.

"Certainly. Like this?"

It's funny how three things can happen in a millisecond, but they can – I've got proof of it on the memory stick of my camera.

Here's what happened, but in slow(er) motion:

• Dylan barged in the back door yelling,

HELP!!

• Fiona jumped out of her skin, flicking flour all over herself.

• My finger automatically hit the shutter in shock.

CLICK!

"What! What's wrong?" asked Fiona, trying to brush flour out of her eyes so she could see her son, and check that all his limbs were there.

"It's an emergency! We need to call Indie's mum! Straight away!"

"Wait – what sort of an emergency?" asked Fiona.

"And why do we need to call Indie's mum?" asked Dad, hobbling painfully into the kitchen.

"Come and see!" urged Dylan, waving us to follow him outside.

And so we hurried round the side of the house, where Dylan suddenly stopped and pointed to Fiona's silver car, parked in the driveway.

Dad – perched on his crutches – stared open-mouthed.

Fiona – lightly dusted white – blinked her floury eyelashes in disbelief.

As for Dylan, he winked at me!

"See?" he said, turning to talk to Dad and Fiona. "We really need to call Indie's mum to help us, don't we?"

"Dylan…" said Dad, very slowly. "What are all those snails doing in the car?"

Beneath the white flour, I was sure Fiona was turning whiter than white. She was certainly swaying, like she might faint at the sight of all those dozens and dozens of garden snails sliming around the inside of her car.

"I don't know!" said Dylan, going a bit pink.

"Well, unless one of them has a spare set of car keys, I think they might have had a bit of help getting in there!" said Dad, frowning.

"I didn't do it, honest!" Dylan protested, going even pinker. "But shouldn't you call Indie's mum now, to rescue them?"

"No – I think you're going to get all of them out of there, Dylan," Dad said, sounding an awful lot like Mum doing her stern voice on me the other day. "And I'm going to take your mother inside and make her some tea while you're doing it."

"But—!" Dylan started to say forlornly, shooting me a look.

"I'll stay and help," I said, sticking my camera on the bonnet of the car. "We're going to need a big bucket…"

One minute and a big bucket later, Dylan and I were inside the car, picking snails from the upholstery like they were raspberries on a bush.

"You did put them in here, didn't you?" I asked my stepbrother, now that we were on our own (apart from the snails).

"Yeah," mumbled Dylan. "Took me ages to collect them all."

(Through the kitchen window, I could see Dad on the phone, holding a copy of the Yellow Pages. "Hello – do you shampoo snail slime out of cars?" I guessed he was saying.)

"But why did you do it?" I asked, thinking that Dylan's mind worked in slantier ways than I'd ever imagined.

"I did it for you."

"What?"

"I did it for you, Indie," Dylan repeated. "I thought it would be a good way of getting your mum over here, and then your parents would be together, on their own, like you wanted."

Yeah, together with several dozen snails, plus me, Dylan and Fiona. It wasn't quite what I had in mind when I asked Dylan for ideas yesterday.

Still, I was pretty touched that he wanted to help me so much.

"I thought it was a really good idea. I thought your mum could rescue the snails and find them new owners, just like Amélie and Fleur."

Yikes! Dylan looked like he might cry.

"It was a really, really good idea," I said, telling my zillionth white lie of the day.

Dylan smiled a watery smile, blissfully unaware that a bunch of snails were crawling back out of the bucket and over his trainers.

The return of the small sad something

Thursday evening.

Everyone from class would have their **family map** projects done by now, ready to take to school tomorrow.

Everyone except me.

141

So far, my family plan was just a pile of stuff scattered on my bedroom floor. Stuff like:

- an A3 sheet of pink card
- a pile of not very good photos (I'd printed out everything on Dylan's computer last night, before Fiona dropped me home – in Dad's car)
- a marker pen.
- some glue

Now all I needed was a bin to put it all in, since I wasn't exactly in the mood to do anything clever with it.

All I was in the mood for was sprawling on my bed, putting my head under the pillow, and staying there for the next ten years.

Tappity-tap-tap.
"Hey, Indie how's the proj— oh!"
It was Caitlin's voice.

"Are you OK?" she asked, sitting down beside me on the bed and putting her hand on my back.

"No," I mumphed, from under my pillow.

"Is it your project?"

"Kind of," I mumphed.

My blue mood; it kind of was my project, but it was especially about my parents not being friends.

"Do you need a hand? I can help you if you like."

I didn't mumph anything. I didn't want any help; I just wanted to be left alone, under my pillow, where it was nice and gloomy and dark.

"Which photos are you going to use? You have to use this one of Dibbles – it's too cute!"

"I don't think we're allowed to include pets," I mumphed.

"Don't be silly!" said Caitlin. "It's a **family map**, and it's up to you to say who's important in your family, right?"

The normal, happy version of Indie would have said, "Yay! You're right!".

Tonight's mumphy version said: "mumph".

"Um, I'll be back in a minute," said Caitlin, getting up off the bed with a pat of my back as she went.

Uh-oh, I really hoped she wasn't going to get her didgeridoo. If she played me anything on that right now, I might just want to stay under this pillow for an extra ten years.

"Indie? What's up, honey?" came a voice, about five minutes later.

Phew, Caitlin hadn't got her didgeridoo, after all. Instead, she'd got my mum.

Though I wasn't in the mood to say much more than "mumph" to her either.

"Do you want to talk?"

"Not really."

"Caitlin says you're a bit upset about your project. Is that right?"

"Mumph."

"Do you want me to do it with you? Would that help?"

"No."

For a few more minutes, Mum tried her best to lure me out from under the pillow, but it just wasn't going to happen.

All I wanted was to be left alone, with my small sad something in my tummy for company.

BING-BONG!

"Back in a sec," said Mum, jumping up to answer the door.

I couldn't hear who was there (especially not with a pillow over my head), but I realized pretty quickly that Mum had left the bedroom door open.

"Oooof!" I grumbled, as a heavy dog (Dibbles), jumped on the bed and flopped down directly on top of me.

KLUNK-stomp. KLUNK-stomp. KLUNK-stomp...

What was that familiar-ish sound?

"India?"

Dad.

It was Dad's voice, and Dad's KLUNK-stomping crutch-steps that I'd heard above Dibbles' contented panting.

What was he doing here?

I wanted to know, but I still didn't want to come out.

"Your mum just called me and asked me to come over."

Well, I guess I knew now.

"What's the problem, Indie? Want to tell Dad?"

Me and my small sad something felt a bit wibbly when we heard Dad say that.

"No," I mumphed, though I sort of wanted to say yes.

I felt a **thump, thump**, as two bottoms sat themselves down on my bed.

"Listen, Indie," I tuned into Mum's voice, to the left of me. "Caitlin just told me … well, what you've been worrying about this last week."

"And on the way here, Dylan explained about all your plans and schemes to get me and your mum talking," said Dad.

"Dylan's here?" I mumphed.

"Well, yes, because Fiona had to drive me over just now."

My heart was thumping wildly – partly because this was getting so weird (I'd wanted to be alone, and now my house was pretty much full), and partly because I was being badly squashed by a very heavy dog.

"Look–"

That was Mum.

"–we understand that you've been unhappy because you think me and Dad aren't friends. But really, it's not true!"

"Mum's right–"

Dad talking, this time.

"–I think we both got in a bad habit of not being nice about each other, just in a jokey way. But we understand now that it's especially not nice for you, Indie."

"And we're not going to do that any more. We promise," said Mum.

WOW. So my parents didn't need white lies about comas and fake texts and the rest to get talking, They just both needed to care about me.

The small sad something in my tummy started fading away. I didn't think I'd miss it too much.

"Indie?" murmured Dad. "Do you want to say anything?"

I wasn't sure I could. I was too stunned with happiness. But finally the right words came...

"Can you get Dibbles off me, please? I can't breathe."

Me and my (mad) family map

"Right, Indie – let's hear from you!" said Miss Levy.

She looked a little frazzled. But then we were all a little frazzled after listening to Simon Green describe his **family map**.

It had gone all right, till it came to the photo of his dad.

Mr Green was dressed in chainmail and armour, at a reconstruction of some hundreds-of-years-ago battle of something. Boy, did Simon Green enjoy telling us the gruesome ways people liked to kill each other in medieval times.

"OK," I said, standing up, and holding my pink piece of card, so the whole class could see.

Soph and Fee beamed up at me. (They'd already done their stuff.

Everyone had "oohed" at Fee's fab poems, and "aahed" at the amount of cousins Soph had.)

> You are the nicest dad
> And you're never, ever mean.
> I love it when you
> make me laugh
> And call me your little
> butterbean.

"Go ahead, Indie," Miss Levy urged me. "This looks very ... interesting!"

Her regular, teacherly smile had slipped. The corners of her mouth were twitching and I reckoned she was trying not to giggle. I think it was 'cause she'd just spotted the oddball photos I'd chosen to use.

Well, I didn't choose them on my own, exactly. Mum and Dad helped last night, along with Caitlin and Dylan and Fiona. (Dibbles didn't help much – Caitlin had to stop him from eating the glue.)

While Mum spread out the photos on the kitchen table, Fiona made tea and juice for everyone, and we all picked our favourites.

Maybe it was 'cause everyone was feeling suddenly giggly and happy, we chose the stupidest: Mum with the paw prints on her face; Dad wiggling his big toe at the camera; Caitlin looking like a wide-mouthed alien; Dylan in deely-boppers and snail shoulder pad. Even Fiona didn't mind me using a photo of her looking floury and messy (at least she said she didn't.)

And there were dumb pictures of the pets too, since my family wouldn't be my family without them.

"Well," I began, as all my classmates listened in, "sometimes people say they live in a madhouse. But I'm lucky, 'cause I get to live in *two* madhouses!"

I pointed to the outline I'd drawn of a house that was supposed to be Mum's, with pictures of Mum, Caitlin and the pets crammed in.

"I love everyone in THIS house," I read out loud, "'cause they are wonderful in an animal-mad, didgeridoo-playing, furry, scaly way!"

Then – using my finger – I followed a silver glitter trail (inspired by my slithery friends, Amélie and Fleur) to the outline of a house that was supposed to be Dad's.

"And I love everyone in THIS house, because they are wonderful in a silly, delicious, deely-bopping way!"

There.

There wasn't as much on my map as there was on some of the other kids'. And what I'd said wasn't as poetic as Fee's poems. But I was pretty pleased with it.

"Very nice. Thank you, Indie. I particularly like the close-up of the dog's nose," smiled Miss Levy.

"That's Dibbles licking the camera," I explained, blushing pinkly.

Dibbles and all the pets ... they were as much a part of my family as my (best of friends) mum and dad. And I couldn't imagine home being home without Caitlin in it, or not having a stepmum as nice as Fiona or a stepbrother as dippy as Dylan.

You know, when Miss Levy first set the **family map** project, I worried about not having a small, happy family.

But I had something much, much better: a big (strange) happy family!